01/2017

Dear Parent:

Congratulations! Your child is taking the first steps on an exciting journey. The destination? Independent reading!

STEP INTO READING® will help your child get there. The program offers five steps to reading success. Each step includes fun stories and colorful art. There are also Step into Reading Sticker Books, Step into Reading Math Readers, Step into Reading Phonics Readers, Step into Reading Write-In Readers, and Step into Reading Phonics Boxed Sets—a complete literacy program with something to interest every child.

Learning to Read, Step by Step!

Ready to Read Preschool–Kindergarten
• big type and easy words • rhyme and rhythm • picture clues
For children who know the alphabet and are eager to begin reading.

Reading with Help Preschool–Grade 1
• basic vocabulary • short sentences • simple stories
For children who recognize familiar words and sound out new words with help.

Reading on Your Own Grades 1–3
• engaging characters • easy-to-follow plots • popular topics
For children who are ready to read on their own.

Reading Paragraphs Grades 2–3
• challenging vocabulary • short paragraphs • exciting stories
For newly independent readers who read simple sentences with confidence.

Ready for Chapters Grades 2–4
• chapters • longer paragraphs • full-color art
For children who want to take the plunge into chapter books but still like colorful pictures.

STEP INTO READING® is designed to give every child a successful reading experience. The grade levels are only guides. Children can progress through the steps at their own speed, developing confidence in their reading, no matter what their grade.

Remember, a lifetime love of reading starts with a single step!

Random House New York

Thomas the Tank Engine & Friends ™ CREATED BY BRITT ALLCROFT
Based on the Railway Series by the Reverend W Awdry.
© 2012, 2017 Gullane (Thomas) LLC.
Thomas the Tank Engine & Friends and Thomas & Friends are trademarks of Gullane (Thomas) Limited. Thomas the Tank Engine & Friends and Design Is Reg. U.S. Pat. & Tm. Off. © 2017 HIT Entertainment Limited. All rights reserved. Published in the United States by Random House Children's Books, a division of Penguin Random House LLC, 1745 Broadway, New York, NY 10019, and in Canada by Penguin Random House Canada Limited, Toronto. Originally published in different form in Great Britain by Egmont UK Ltd., as *Buzzy Bees*, in 2012.

Step into Reading, Random House, and the Random House colophon are registered trademarks of Penguin Random House LLC.

Visit us on the Web!
StepIntoReading.com
randomhousekids.com
www.thomasandfriends.com

ISBN 978-0-399-55770-5 (trade) — ISBN 978-0-399-55771-2 (lib. bdg.) — ISBN 978-0-399-55772-9 (ebook)

Printed in the United States of America
10 9 8 7 6 5 4 3 2 1

HiT entertainment

STEP INTO READING®

STEP 2

READING WITH HELP

THOMAS & FRIENDS™

Thomas and the BUZZY BEES

Based on the Railway Series
by the Reverend W Awdry

Thomas has
a special job.
He will carry
a load of beehives!

Hiro tells Thomas

to go slow.

The bees need
to rest.

Thomas puffs past
a field of flowers.
He thinks
the bees will like
the flowers.

Thomas hears
buzzing.
The bees are
leaving
their hives!

Thomas picks up
a new load.
These trucks are
full of flowers.
The bees fly back
to Thomas.

The bees fly
all around Thomas.

Now they are
too close!

Thomas leaves all of
the trucks behind.
He rolls away
from the bees.

Thomas meets Hiro
on the track.
Hiro is looking for
the flowers
and the bees.

Thomas knows

he did not do his job.

Thomas picks up
the flowers.
He picks up
the hives.
The bees follow.

Thomas puffs along
a shady track.

The bees feel cool.
They fly back
into the beehives.

The buzzy bees
are home
on the farm
at last!